SAN FRANCISCO

SAN FRANCISCO

SAN FRANCISCO

SAN FRANCISCO

SAN FRANCISCO $8.99

SAN FRANCISCO

SAN FRANCISCO

SAN FRANCISCO

SAN FRANCISCO

SAN FRANCISCO

TO:

FROM:

SAN FRANCISCO

SAN FRANCISCO

SAN FRANCISCO

SAN FRANCISCO

SAN FRANCISCO

SAN FRANCISCO

SAN FRANCISCO

SAN FRANCISCO

SAN FRANCISCO

SAN FRANCISCO

SAN FRANCISCO $8.99

Published by Sourcebooks Wonderland, an imprint of Sourcebooks Kids
P.O. Box 4410, Naperville, Illinois 60567-4410
(630) 961-3900
sourcebookskids.com

Library of Congress Cataloging-in-Publication Data is on file with the publisher.

Source of Production: 1010 Printing Asia Limited, North Point, Hong Kong, China
Date of Production: May 2019
Run Number: 5014980

Printed and bound in China.
OGP 10 9 8 7 6 5 4 3 2 1

HIDE AND SEEK
SAN FRANCISCO

BY ERIN GUENDELSBERGER   PICTURES BY MATTIA CERATO

sourcebooks
wonderland

FISHERMAN'S WHARF

MUIR WOODS
NATIONAL MONUMENT

SAN FRANCISCO
INTERNATIONAL AIRPORT

UNION SQUARE

OCEAN BEACH

THE SAN FRANCISCO ZOO

GOLDEN GATE PARK

FERRY BUILDING
MARKETPLACE

AQUARIUM OF THE BAY

THE CALIFORNIA
ACADEMY OF SCIENCES

3

FISHERMAN'S WHARF

FISHERMAN'S WHARF is the home of San Francisco Bay's fishing fleet. Most fishing boats today belong to the **THIRD GENERATION** of fishing craft, diesel-powered boats. The first generation boats, used from the 1840s through the early 1900s, were sailboats without motors. Second generation fishing boats were small, gas engine boats. **FISHERMAN'S WHARF** was built on top of debris from other buildings after the earthquake and fire of 1906.

Visitors to Fisherman's Wharf can shop, eat famous **DUNGENESS CRABS**, and enjoy many types of entertainment. There are museums, an aquarium, a WWII ship and submarine, a carousel, musical stairs, a mirror maze, and more. At **PIER 39**, sea lions rest and play. Ferries leave from Fisherman's Wharf to visit **ALCATRAZ ISLAND**, the site of a prison that once confined well-known criminals like **AL CAPONE**!

CAN YOU FIND...

THE WATERFRONT SHOP

PIER 39

STCARDS-SOUVENIRS

RESTAURANT

NOW THAT YOU'RE HERE, COULD YOU HELP ME FIND A FEW OTHER ITEMS?

FERRY BUILDING MARKETPLACE

The **FERRY BUILDING MARKETPLACE** is a gathering spot for local farmers, artisan producers, and independent food businesses in San Francisco. After opening in 1898, it became a primary portal into the city. Until the 1930s, most travelers and commuters to the city had to come by **FERRY**. But by the 1940s, with the opening of the **BAY BRIDGE** and **GOLDEN GATE BRIDGE**, travelers could reach the city by car and the ferry was used very little. The **FERRY BUILDING** was no longer used and was converted into office space. In the early 2000s, however, the marketplace was restored, reopening in 2003.

Today, the Ferry Building is a world-class public food market with merchants selling food, beverages, groceries, sweets, and more. Visitors can shop, dine at restaurants and cafés, and visit a farmers market. About **40,000** shoppers visit the farmers market each week.

CAN YOU FIND...

THE CALIFORNIA ACADEMY OF SCIENCES

The **CALIFORNIA ACADEMY OF SCIENCES** was founded in 1853 to showcase California's wonders. First visitors could see a woolly mammoth, grizzly bears, native plants, and artifacts. Unfortunately, the great San Francisco earthquake and fire of 1906 destroyed most of the academy's specimens, and the academy moved to **GOLDEN GATE PARK** in 1916. After another earthquake in 1989, the museum was redesigned to bring all exhibits under one roof, which opened in 2008.

The academy's Institute for Biodiversity Science and Sustainability has almost **46 MILLION SPECIMENS**, one of the largest collections in the world. The planetarium has a seventy-five-foot-tall dome, and the aquarium is home to nearly **40,000 LIVE ANIMALS**. Visitors can also explore a four-story rainforest and exhibits about earthquakes, coral reefs, animals, dinosaurs, gems, minerals, and even a swamp exhibit with an albino alligator named **CLAUDE**!

CAN YOU FIND...

WOW, THERE'S A LOT HERE! CAN YOU HELP ME FIND THESE THINGS?

MUIR WOODS NATIONAL MONUMENT

PRESIDENT THEODORE ROOSEVELT created Muir Woods National Monument in 1908. Until the 1800s, large REDWOOD TREES covered many of northern California's coastal valleys. Because loggers cut down most of these trees, Congressman William Kent bought 611 acres of one of the area's last stands of old-growth redwoods in 1905. Kent and his wife donated 295 acres to the government, which became MUIR WOODS, the seventh U.S. national monument, named after conservationist JOHN MUIR.

Today, Muir Woods contains six miles of hiking trails where visitors can see old-growth coast redwoods, the tallest living things in the world! These redwoods range from 400 to 800 YEARS OLD and can be as tall as 250 FEET. Muir Woods has a variety of flora and fauna, including more than fifty species of birds, like spotted owls and pileated woodpeckers.

CAN YOU FIND...

CAN YOU ALSO LOOK FOR THESE THINGS?

GOLDEN GATE PARK

GOLDEN GATE PARK, the third-most visited park in the United States, was developed in the 1870s. Trees were planted across the land's original sand dunes, and by 1879, the park had 155,000 trees. Several **WINDMILLS** were constructed in 1905 to pump water throughout the park. At one time, moose, antelope, zebras, elephants, ostriches, and peacocks walked the grounds. These animals were eventually moved to new homes, but there are still bison at the **BUFFALO PADDOCK**.

Golden Gate Park is over three miles long, encompassing more than **1,000 ACRES**. About **13 MILLION PEOPLE** visit the park each year to see its majestic meadows, groves, lakes, and attractions. Park visitors can also enjoy a Japanese tea garden, arboretum, aquarium, conservatory of flowers, and carousel, as well as the **DEYOUNG MUSEUM** and the **CALIFORNIA ACADEMY OF SCIENCES**.

CAN YOU FIND...

NOW THAT YOU'RE HERE, WOULD YOU MIND HELPING ME FIND A FEW OTHER ITEMS?

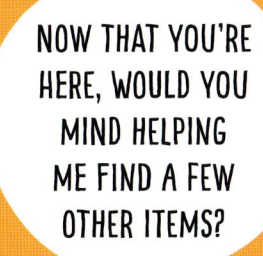

x2

AQUARIUM OF THE BAY

The **AQUARIUM OF THE BAY**, located on the waterfront at **PIER 39**, has 700,000 gallons of bay water and approximately **20,000 MARINE ANIMALS** native to the San Francisco Bay and nearby waters. The aquarium first opened in 1996, and seven million guests have visited over its twenty-year history. The aquarium is dedicated to the diverse marine life of the area and aims to restore and protect the **SAN FRANCISCO BAY**.

Visitors to the aquarium can see octopuses, jellyfish, otters, sea stars, rays, guitarfish, and more. San Francisco Bay's largest predator, the **SEVENGILL SHARK**, is on display, as are white sturgeons, the largest freshwater fish in North America. White sturgeons can be as big as twelve feet long and eleven hundred pounds! Daily shark, otter, and bat ray feedings are open for public viewing, and visitors can touch sharks, rays, and sea stars.

CAN YOU FIND...

$8.99

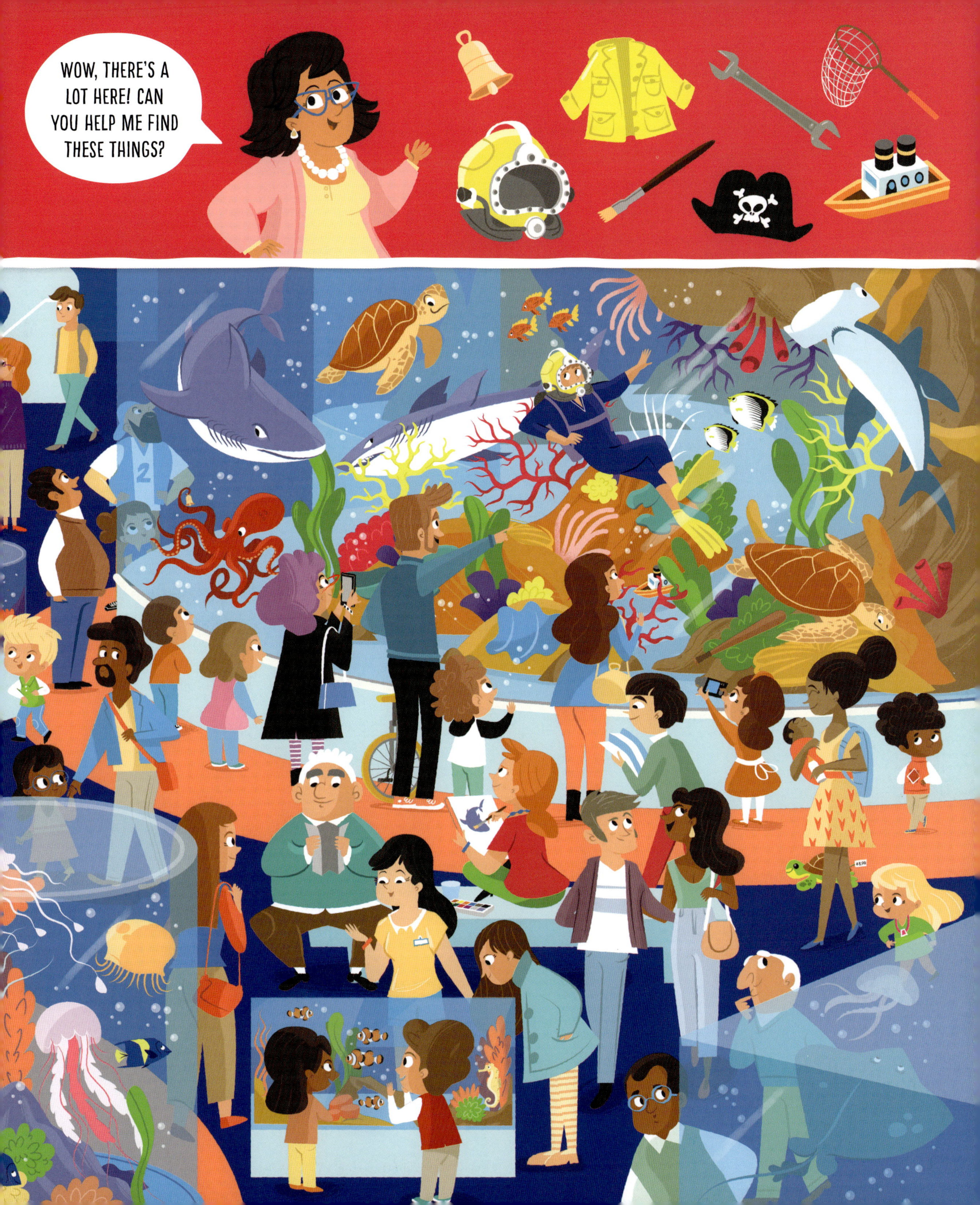
WOW, THERE'S A LOT HERE! CAN YOU HELP ME FIND THESE THINGS?

UNION SQUARE

Built in 1850, **UNION SQUARE** was where pro-Union demonstrations were held right before the **CIVIL WAR**. The park was named to commemorate these rallies. At that time, the square was basically a large sand hill, with land sloping down toward **MARKET STREET**. Eventually the land was leveled out and **UNION SQUARE** was formally designed as a park. **HORSE-DRAWN CARS** ran up and down the streets in the early 1870s, and **CABLE CARS** were introduced around 1877. The **DEWEY MONUMENT** was dedicated by President Theodore Roosevelt on May 14, 1903, commemorating a major victory in the **SPANISH-AMERICAN WAR**. Much of Union Square was rebuilt after the earthquake and fire that struck San Francisco in 1906.

Today, the twenty-seven-block Union Square district has restaurants, shops, hotels, art galleries, salons, and theaters, and hosts festivals and other events throughout the year.

CAN YOU FIND...

WHILE YOU'RE HERE, CAN YOU ALSO FIND THESE OBJECTS?

OCEAN BEACH

Before the late 1800s, what is now **OCEAN BEACH** was separated from San Francisco by a "vast sand-dune wilderness." Eventually, a **STEAM RAILROAD** allowed access to the beach, and development started. Between 1850 and 1926, dozens of ships were wrecked along **OCEAN BEACH**, and the hull of the **KING PHILIP**, which ran aground in 1878, can still be seen during very low tides.

Beach visitors today enjoy a 3.5-mile stretch of white sand and dunes facing the **PACIFIC OCEAN**, a paved path for walkers and cyclists, and the historic **CLIFF HOUSE** restaurant. The once-popular **SUTRO BATHS** are closed, but visitors can explore the **RUINS** of the baths. While it's not a good idea to swim at Ocean Beach because of the dangerous rip currents and frigid water temperatures, experienced surfers wearing wet suits do hit the waves.

CAN YOU FIND...

CAN YOU ALSO LOOK FOR THESE THINGS?

x4

SAN FRANCISCO INTERNATIONAL AIRPORT

After leasing **150 ACRES** of pastureland from a banker, the City and County of San Francisco dedicated the **MILLS FIELD MUNICIPAL AIRPORT** of San Francisco in 1927. In the early 1930s, the airport hosted air shows and hangar dances that attracted many visitors. At the outbreak of WWII in the Pacific, the U.S. military took control of the airport, and it temporarily became a **U.S. ARMY AIR CORPS** training and staging facility.

After the war, the airport transitioned back to public use. The number of passengers using the airport has increased through the years—with one million annual passengers by 1948, 10 million by 1966, 20 million by 1981, and more than 55 million by 2017. Visitors today can enjoy art exhibits as well as the **AVIATION MUSEUM AND LIBRARY**, which opened in 2010.

CAN YOU FIND...

GATES

DUTY FREE

DUTY

50%

DEPARTURES
TIME	DESTINATION	FLIGHT #	GATE
10:15	BERLIN	A7889	12
10:25	PORTLAND	B3612	34
11:00	ROME	Z9000	04
11:05	CALGARY	D2145	10
11:45	MEXICO CITY	U8998	03
12:00	MIAMI	A2098	09
12:25	SYDNEY	B4567	45

EXIT

Mr. Lee

BLUE BIRD COMPANY

NOW THAT YOU'RE HERE, COULD YOU HELP ME FIND A FEW OTHER ITEMS?

THE SAN FRANCISCO ZOO

The **SAN FRANCISCO ZOO** started with a single California **GRIZZLY BEAR**. In 1889, a reporter captured a live grizzly to prove they were not extinct. **MONARCH THE BEAR** became a proud symbol of California and the city's commitment to conservation. Monarch inspired **HERBERT FLEISCHHACKER** to pursue his dream of creating a zoo. In 1922, Fleischhacker bought land in the southwest corner of San Francisco, where the zoo remains today. The zoo's first big exhibits included **MONKEY ISLAND**, a lion house, an elephant house, and bear grottoes.

Today, the San Francisco Zoo has over **2,000 ANIMALS** from **250 UNIQUE SPECIES**. Visitors can see big cats, bears, giraffes, zebras, gorillas, rhinoceroses, reptiles, birds, and more. Families can also enjoy a petting zoo or ride the **HISTORIC 1921 CAROUSEL** and the **1904 LITTLE PUFFER STEAM TRAIN**.

CAN YOU FIND...

WHILE YOU'RE HERE, CAN YOU ALSO FIND THESE OBJECTS?